This book belongs to:

_____

_____

_____

First published 2002 by Walker Books Ltd
87 Vauxhall Walk, London SE11 5HJ

This edition published 2004

2 4 6 8 10 9 7 5 3 1

© 2002 Lucy Cousins
Lucy Cousins font © 2002 Lucy Cousins
The author/illustrator has asserted her moral rights

Based on the Audio Visual series "Maisy". A King Rollo Films production for
Universal Pictures International Visual Programming. Original script by Andrew Brenner.
Illustrated in the style of Lucy Cousins by King Rollo Films Ltd.

Maisy™. Maisy is a registered trademark of Walker Books Ltd, London.

Printed in Hong Kong

All rights reserved

British Library Cataloguing in Publication Data:
a catalogue record for this book is
available from the British Library

0-7445-8945-2

www.walkerbooks.co.uk

Maisy Tidies Up

Lucy Cousins

WALKER BOOKS
AND SUBSIDIARIES

LONDON · BOSTON · SYDNEY · AUCKLAND

Maisy is cleaning her house today.

Ding-dong!
Oh, who can that be?

It's Charley!
Come in, Charley.
You're just in time
to help Maisy
tidy up.

Charley can smell something delicious.

What's that in the kitchen, Maisy?

Lots of yummy cakes!

Oh dear, the floor is still wet.
You'll have to wait until it's dry, Charley.

While he's waiting,
Charley tidies
up all the toys.

And Maisy vacuums
the sitting room.

Then Charley cleans the windows from the inside...

And Maisy cleans them from the outside.

That looks better!

At last the kitchen
floor is dry.
Now Maisy and
Charley can have
some cakes.
Hooray!

Well done, Maisy.
Well done, Charley.
Enjoy your cakes.